Haldane, Suzanne

Painting faces

PAINTING FACES

PAINTING

FACES

SUZANNE HALDANE

E. P. DUTTON NEW YORK

for Vincent T. Brandeis and Neils H. Lauersen, who are doing their part to add young readers to the world

My sincere thanks for the generous assistance of the following people:
Kristen Angarola; Jean Brock; Jaspar Carrington; Jason Cetrano; Sean Dunn;
James C. Faris, University of Connecticut; Lawrence Glickman, principal of South
Orangetown Middle School; Brina Gredzinski; Avril James; Olivia Johnson;
Lt. Col. Paul Knox, U.S. Army Public Affairs; Michael and Mindy Lampell;
Willy Mercado; Andrew and Benjamin Moore; C.R.V. Rao, India Government
Tourist Office; Bryan Roberts; Marti Robinson; Marcia Seskin; D.J. Sta. Ana;
Elizabeth and Gina Trincellito; and Kari Webber.

Library of Congress Cataloging-in-Publication Data
Haldane, Suzanne.
    Painting faces.
    Summary: Text and color photographs introduce
painted faces from various cultures and countries.
Also included are directions that children can
follow for painting some of them.
    1. Face painting—Juvenile literature. I. Title.
TT911.H35 1988 745.5 88-3706
ISBN 0-525-44408-4

Published in the United States by
E. P. Dutton, a division of
Penguin Books USA Inc.

Published simultaneously in Canada by
Fitzhenry & Whiteside Limited, Toronto

Printed in Hong Kong by South China Printing Co.
First Edition   W   10 9 8 7 6 5 4 3

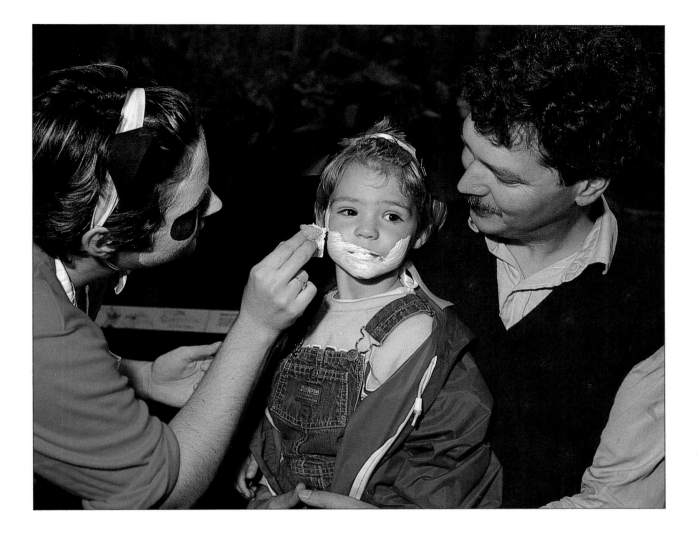

Hearts, flowers, diamonds, zigzags. Suns, moons, stars, Halley's comet. Any shape or pattern you can imagine has probably been painted on someone's face at some time or other.

For thousands of years, around the world, people have felt the need to decorate their faces. The reasons why are as varied as the languages people speak. Sometimes people have painted their faces to establish kinship with animals or gods, to signal that they are celebrating or mourning, or to kindle feelings of bravery, beauty, or love. But whatever the reason, a face smeared with colored clay, or styled with modern liners, blushes, and powders, seems to release energy and imagination in the wearer.

Native American Iroquois

Southeast Nuba (from Africa)

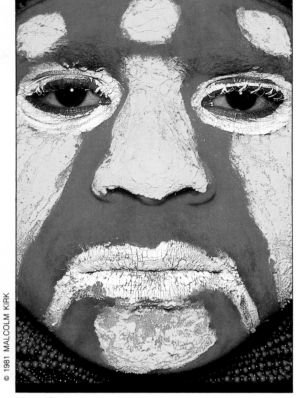

New Guinea

Chinese opera

Somewhere on nearly every continent there are people who paint their faces. Some of the most interesting and original designs are made by people who live in very isolated societies, often on remote islands or tucked away in the mountains, far from the modern world. Exciting faces can be found, too, in the traditional theater of Asia.

Kabuki-style makeup worn by actors
in the production *Shogun Macbeth*

Bali

Nepal

Kathakali (from India)

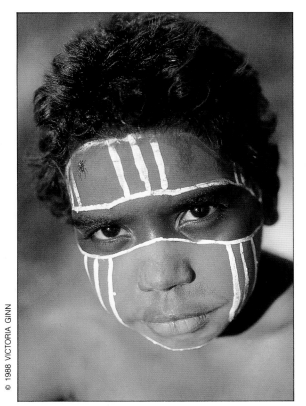

Australia

Halloween is a holiday when many people in this country, children especially, paint their faces. But it doesn't have to be Halloween for you to see a painted face. Football fans sometimes smear their team's colors on their skin; St. Patrick's Day celebrants paint shamrocks on their cheeks and dye their hair green; enthusiastic sunbathers apply colorful zinc-oxide compounds to protect them from sunburn. Face painting is one of the most popular activities at fairs and carnivals. And many women use face makeup every day to make themselves more beautiful.

Face painting is sometimes even part of a person's job. Actors and actresses use makeup to exaggerate their features under the harsh lights of theater or film. Or they use it to change their appearances drastically. Football and baseball players draw thick lines of black greasepaint under their eyes to absorb strong sunlight and prevent glare. And United States Army recruits learn how to apply camouflage makeup to their faces.

There are lots of painted faces in this book. The faces on pages 6–9 are those of authentic native peoples or performers. The young people on pages 15–32 are American schoolchildren. Some of the designs they display are based on those worn by people in other cultures and countries. Some are inspired by animals. And some were painted by the wearers themselves, using their own imagination.

Directions are given for the easiest way to make many of the faces. Follow the directions or let what you see inspire you to create your own design.

Long ago, people made face paint by grinding colored stones or various clays, then mixing them with vegetable oil or animal fat. Sometimes they used plants to make colors. They ground up roots, then mixed them with fat; or they boiled leaves in water, dried them, then crushed them into a powder and mixed the powder with oil.

For designing your face, you *must* use makeup that has been specially produced for applying to your skin. Any other substances are likely to cause irritation. Do *not* use watercolor crayons, watercolors, finger paints, felt-tipped markers, poster paints, oil paints, or any coloring that has not been made to put on your face.

Zinc-oxide sunburn protection

Baseball player Bucky Dent

U.S. Army camouflage

Christine Langer in
the Broadway musical *Cats*

You may already have everyday makeup in your house that can be used to make some of the faces in this book. Colorful eye shadows come in cream or stick form; lipsticks are available in pink, red, orange, purple, and other colors; and eyeliner pencils, which are good for outlining a design, come in brown, green, blue, black, and gray.

There are two kinds of makeup made especially for painting faces: water-based makeup and greasepaint. Each allows the skin to breathe and has been tested to minimize the possibility of irritating sensitive skin. And each comes in brighter and more exciting colors than the makeup made to be worn every day.

But because each person's skin is different, it is a good idea to test makeup before using it on your face. Smear a little on the inside of your wrist, wait an hour, then wash it off. If there is no redness on your skin, it is safe to apply the makeup to your face.

Before you begin, tuck a few paper towels around your neck to protect your clothes. Or if you have an old long-sleeved shirt, tie the sleeves around your neck to make a giant bib.

Find some way of keeping your hair away from your face until you finish making up. Bobby pins, an old scarf, or styling mousse work well.

Water-based makeup is easy to use. It brushes on smoothly, doesn't feel heavy or greasy on your skin, and comes off with soap and water. It is sold in plastic bottles or tubes, ready to use. Sometimes it comes in either a boxed set that looks like a watercolor paint box or in separate round, flat tins. For either of these, you must dip a brush into water before you use each color. Have two containers of water handy: one for wetting your brush and cleaning it when you change colors; the other to be kept clean for erasing your mistakes with tissues or cotton swabs. If you need to correct an error, dip a cotton swab into water and then in a bit of soap before you rub off your mistake.

Greasepaint is more solid and covers the skin more densely than some water-based makeup, which can be streaky. Sometimes the colors available are more vivid. Before putting greasepaint on, you *must* thoroughly rub a thin layer of cold cream into your skin. The cream protects your skin and makes it easy to remove the greasepaint when you're finished.

Greasepaint comes in sticks, tubes, pencils, crayons, or cakes. There are many ways to apply it. You can dab it on, then smooth it over large areas of skin with your fingers. You can roll one end of a cotton swab in it, then use the swab for drawing lines on your face. If the paint is in stick or pencil form, you can draw directly on your face. After you have made up with greasepaint, it's a good idea, but not essential, to pat your face with transparent face powder. Using a fairly large, soft makeup brush or a large wad of cotton, lightly brush off excess powder. The powder sets the makeup and reduces shine. To remove greasepaint, smear cold cream on your face. Wipe everything off with tissues or paper towels, then wash your face with soap and water.

To remove either kind of makeup from near your eyes, always wipe in a direction away from your eyes.

All the faces shown on pages 15–32 of this book have been made with water-based makeup, except the Southeast Nuba face, which was done with greasepaint. It's a good idea to use only one form of makeup in the same design, because water and grease don't mix.

To paint your face you will need:

water-based makeup or greasepaint
box of facial tissues
bobby pins, old scarf,
    or styling mousse
    (to keep hair away from face)
paper towels
cotton swabs

for water-based makeup:
2 small containers of water
2 or 3 watercolor brushes
    (⅜" flat brush,
    #2 and #4 round brushes)

for greasepaint:
jar of cold cream
transparent face powder
powder puff
soft ½" makeup brush
    or a large wad of cotton

Water-based makeup

Greasepaint

NATIVE AMERICAN

Long ago, Native Americans in the United States and Canada painted their faces for many reasons. Hunters applied color as camouflage. Young men often painted their faces before sporting competitions. Warriors decorated themselves before battle to appear fierce, and after battle to remind others of their bravery. Members of many tribes mourned the loss of dead relatives by adding certain colors to their faces.

Face paint had an additional benefit, too. It protected the wearer from the harsh effects of wind and sun.

Native Americans made paint by grinding ingredients from plants and the earth in mortars, or by rubbing them on flat stones. They mixed the resulting powder with water or animal fat and applied the color with their hands or with a reed that had been pounded or chewed until its end became a flat, crude brush. Sometimes they even put liquid paint in their mouths and sprayed the colors on each other.

Today, Native Americans usually use commercially prepared face paint if they decorate themselves for special ceremonies.

Making the Native American Faces

Upper left: During the late 1800s, in the Canadian province of British Columbia, the Haida people often painted realistic images, like this sun, between the eyes or over the lower part of the nose and the entire mouth.
- First paint the red circle, then carefully add the black rays.

Upper right: Another Haida design depicts a hawk's tail.
- Begin by painting the red feathers, then add black to the tips.

Lower left: This green design was worn by an Oto man from southeast Nebraska.

- Choose a lime green and start the design anywhere on your face you like.

Lower right: The wife of a celebrated hunter wore this design. She was a Cree. Her people lived in the Canadian provinces of Saskatchewan and Manitoba.
- This design, too, you can begin anywhere you like.

On page 6 you can see a design made by an Iroquois man.

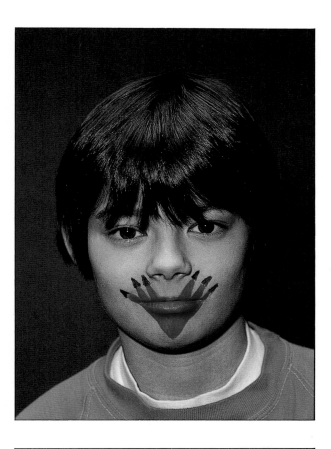
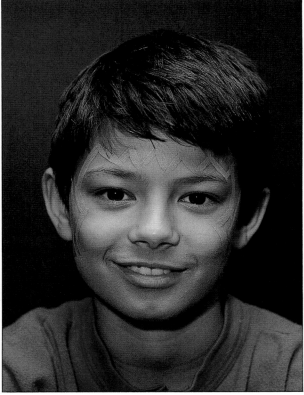
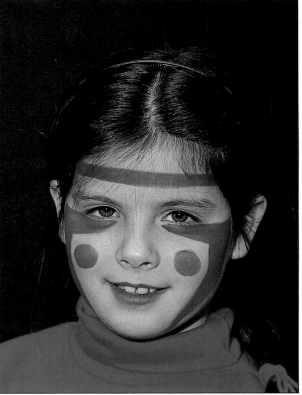

HUICHOL

The Huichol people are Native Americans who live high in the mountains of southwestern Mexico. They are known for the extraordinary fabric designs they embroider with brightly colored yarns.

For a long time, corn—or maize—has been an essential part of the Huichol diet. They make drinks, cereal, bread, cakes, tortillas, and tamales from it. Religious ceremonies are often built around the planting and harvesting of maize. During such fiestas, the Huichol paint their faces.

Yellow is the color they most often use. The root of the uxa plant, which is a kind of small bush, is ground and made into a paste. The Huichol dip pieces of straw into the color and apply the paint. Like their fabric designs, Huichol face designs can be quite complex.

Making the Huichol Face

This pattern represents cornfields and clouds. On the forehead and chin, the barbed lines signify clouds. The lines on the cheeks and nose are the boundaries of fields; the dots between the boundaries stand for corn.

- Choose a yellow that shows up well on your face.
- Paint all the lines first.
- Add the dots.

KATHAKALI

From the southwest coast of India comes a unique kind of theater known as Kathakali. The word *katha* means "story," and the word *kali* means "play." Kathakali performances are story-plays that blend dance and drama.

Many centuries old, the plots of Kathakali dance-dramas are drawn from myths and legends. Quite a few of the characters are gods and demons. Such supernatural beings require a special makeup worthy of their power. Consequently, Kathakali makeup is a fantastic mix of design and color. Audiences familiar with the roles in a dance-drama can identify characters by the patterns and colors on the dancers' faces.

Kathakali dancers usually have their makeup applied by someone else. Each day the makeup artist prepares fresh paint by grinding blue, green, orange, yellow, red, and black stones into fine powders. Coconut oil is added to the powder, and then it is applied to the dancer's face with a long, thin piece of bamboo. Because it takes as long as four hours to make up some Kathakali faces, the dancer lies comfortably on the floor while being made up.

Making the Kathakali Face

- Paint a white line from one ear across the chin to the other ear—a kind of beard.
- Carefully paint the exaggerated, sweeping black lines around your eyes. And don't forget the two black marks on the forehead.
- Paint your lips red, and draw a large round dot on either side of your mouth.
- Add the bannerlike design on your forehead in orange, and then color in the arrowhead shape with yellow.
- Fill all empty spaces with green. You can paint your nose green or white.

A green nose denotes a traditional character called Krishna—a god from stories based on the Hindu religion. The model at right chose a white nose to make the design more colorful. He holds his hand in a Kathakali gesture that represents a deer.

See page 9 for another example of a Kathakali face.

18

CHINESE OPERA

Chinese opera is thousands of years old, and may have been influenced by ancient Indian theater.

Although there are many stories in Chinese opera, there are only fourteen types of roles for actors to play. Heroes, villains, comics, gods, women—whatever the character, each fits into a category, and each category has its own style of makeup. The most extraordinary designs are called *lien p'u,* "the face that shows a record," in which the makeup indicates the true nature of the character. There is a popular legend to explain how *lien p'u* makeup originated.

In the early days of China, a prince named Chang Kung was known for his bravery. Even so, he felt inadequate because he had a slender body and a feminine face. To appear more fearsome, the prince had a frightening mask made, which he wore in battle; thereafter he always led his men to victory.

It's probable that in early operas portraying the life of Chang Kung, some of the actors wore masks. But as time went on, the actors began to paint the masks directly onto their faces.

The *lien p'u* designs still have a masklike appearance—they hide the structure of the actor's face. Eyes, nose, and mouth are painted over as if they didn't exist.

Making the Chinese Opera Face

The sad face at right is a character called Peach Blossom from Chinese opera.
- Carefully draw brown outlines around your eyes; don't forget the tear on each side of the nose.
- Fill in the large brown areas.
- Paint a red, turned-down mouth over your own.
- Next use orange on the bottom of your chin, and make scrolling lines around the outside edges of your eyes and on your forehead.
- On the lower portion of your cheeks and in the middle of your forehead, add a circle of six round dots, and place one dot in the middle of each circle.
- Fill in all around with green.

Turn to page 7 for another example of a Chinese opera face.

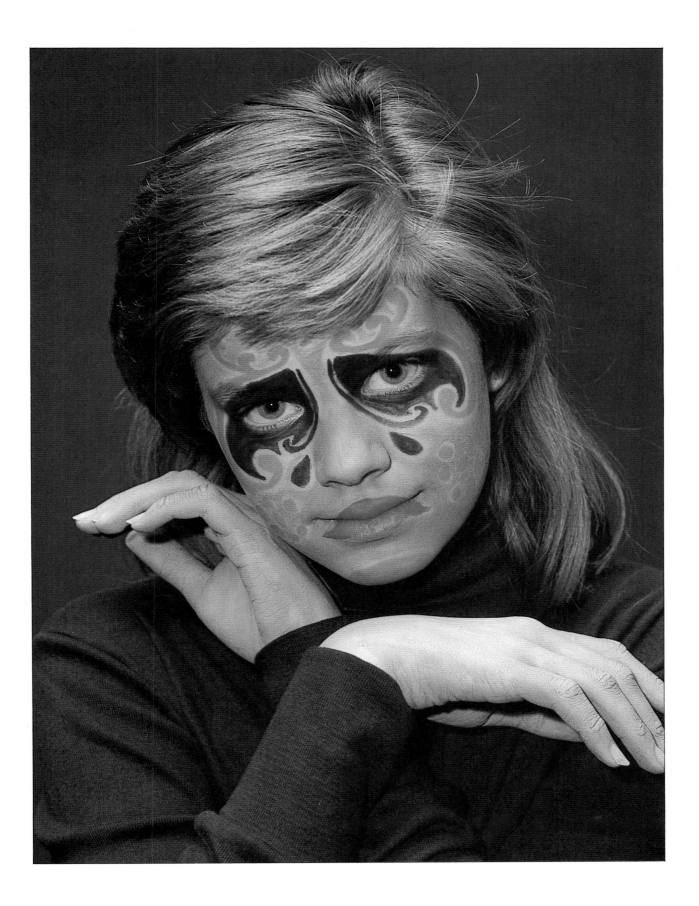

21

KABUKI

The face at right is a design from Kabuki, a type of Japanese theater that dates back to 1586. A century later, an actor named Ichikawa Danjuro I created the stylized Kabuki makeup known as *kumadori*. Although he was influenced by the painted faces of Chinese opera, kumadori designs are simpler and follow the structure of the actor's face.

Kumadori is reserved for male heroes, villains, gods, and demons. Those actors playing women and young men paint their faces white and use little or no other color.

The word *kumadori* means ''pattern taking.'' When an actor applies his makeup, he is said to draw lines of color on his face that trace the pattern, or route, the blood takes as it flows through his veins in a characteristic emotion. Many designs express anger and power. Kumadori faces look rather fierce and tense as a result. A hero of a play who must correct some injustice wears makeup that shows the anger he is feeling inside, as the pattern on the face at right does.

The Kabuki actor applies his makeup himself, using fine brushes or his fingers, depending on the area he is painting. Young boys have their fathers make them up.

Making the Kabuki Kumadori Face

- Draw red lines on your face as shown at right, beginning with your forehead.
- Above each eyebrow, draw a sweeping black line.
- Draw black lines under each eye. Note how the line dips down in the inside corner of each eye. Paint black on your upper lip, too.

- Carefully fill in between all lines with white.

On pages 8–9 you can see other examples of Kabuki faces.

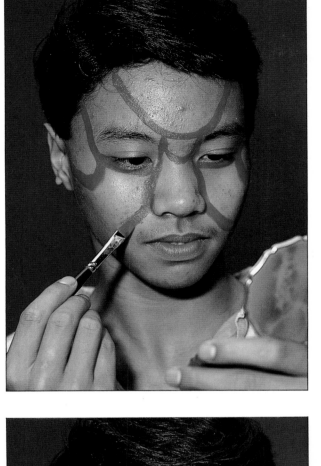

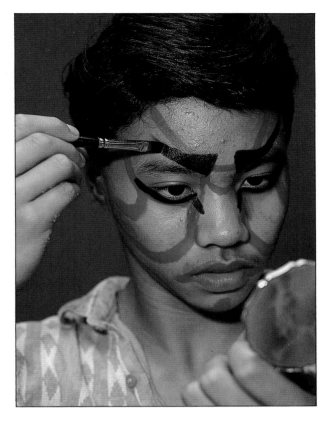

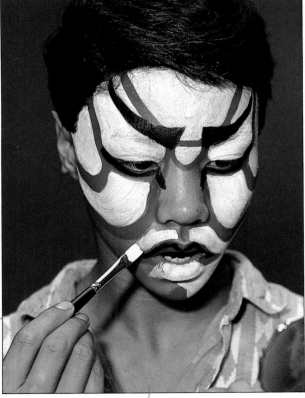

SOUTHEAST NUBA

In the remote mountains of the Sudan, a country in northeast Africa, there is a small group of people called Southeast Nuba, who paint their faces in intricate designs. They have probably never seen the canvases of modern artists, but their artistic achievement is every bit as grand.

Only men design their faces. They consider it a challenge to paint their faces each day in the most artistic way possible. A good effort is praised. The maker of a poor attempt is encouraged to wipe his face clean and try again. Because a Southeast Nuba is trying to make himself look handsome, he makes a pattern that enhances his good features while minimizing the less attractive parts of his face. Sometimes he is inspired by the animals he knows. Antelopes, giraffes, leopards, birds, and small savanna deer frequently show up as design elements.

Strict rules govern Nuba face painting. A young man, for example, is allowed only a limited choice of color until he reaches about age twenty. Men older than forty-five stop painting their faces altogether. Face painting is considered a privilege of the young.

Young women smear a broad blanket of color on their faces but do not create elaborate designs. And newborn children have either red or yellow paint rubbed on their heads.

A Southeast Nuba first applies sesame or peanut oil to his skin. Then he dusts color onto the oil. For drawing details he uses a piece of straw dipped into a different color. Stripes or spots are made with his fingertips.

Making the Southeast Nuba Face

This design was inspired by an African bird.
- Use black to draw a large triangle over each eye and down your cheeks.
- Before filling in the triangle with black, divide the shape in two, leaving a half-inch space down the center.

- Next take gold or a yellow-brown and fill in all empty spaces.

See page 7 for another Southeast Nuba face.

ANIMAL FACES

Designs inspired by animals appear in the art and theater of many different cultures. People all over the world like to paint their faces to resemble animals. You can try making those at right, or you can design your face to look like an animal you know—your pet, for instance.

Making Animal Faces

Upper left—leopard:
- Paint black lines around your eyes.
- Fill in the area with white.
- Put some black on the end of your nose and down along each side.
- Draw a black line from the base of your nose to your upper lip, then add black to your top lip and a little to the middle of the lower one.
- Add black whiskers, and then spots.
- Fill all empty spaces with yellow.

Upper right—monkey:
- Carefully outline your eyes in black, and then in white.
- Use black again, right next to the white, curving up, over, and around it.
- In the middle of your forehead, draw another black line that echoes the one around your eyes.
- Make the tip of your nose black and draw a thick line from under your nose to your upper lip.
- Color your upper lip black, then add a little to the middle of your lower lip.
- Fill the empty spaces with brown.

Lower left—butterfly:
- Using black, draw the butterfly's body by making a line from your forehead, a little above your nose, down to your upper lip.
- Draw the head and antennas on your forehead.
- Draw the upper wings around your eyes. You can style them any way you like.
- To make the lower wings, draw a black line around your cheeks and end the lines halfway under your bottom lip.
- Fill in the wings with any color or colors you like.

Lower right—panda:
- Carefully draw large black patches around your eyes, then fill them in.
- Paint the tip of your nose black.
- Draw a line from the base of your nose to your upper lip, and paint your upper lip black.
- Fill in all around with white.

CLOWN

Clowns in various parts of the world have different ways of making up their faces. But the most familiar type of clown makeup is whiteface—a white face with red and black markings. The white base is thought to have originated in France in the 1600s. A couple of comic players, who were former bakers, greased their faces with animal fat, then dabbed white flour onto the grease, creating their own kind of makeup.

In 1860, a more convenient way of creating a white face was invented. Animal fat and chalk were combined to form what we now call greasepaint.

A clown's makeup is a personal trademark. Each clown welcomes the chance to create his or her original design.

Making the Clown Face

- Carefully draw a black line above and below the middle of each eye.
- Extend lines out from the top and bottom to meet about an inch beyond the outer corner of the eye.
- Fill in the triangle shape you've made with black.
- Take red and make three upside-down teardrops in the middle of your forehead.
- Color your lips red also.
- Add a large pink round spot on each cheek.
- Fill in around the design with white.

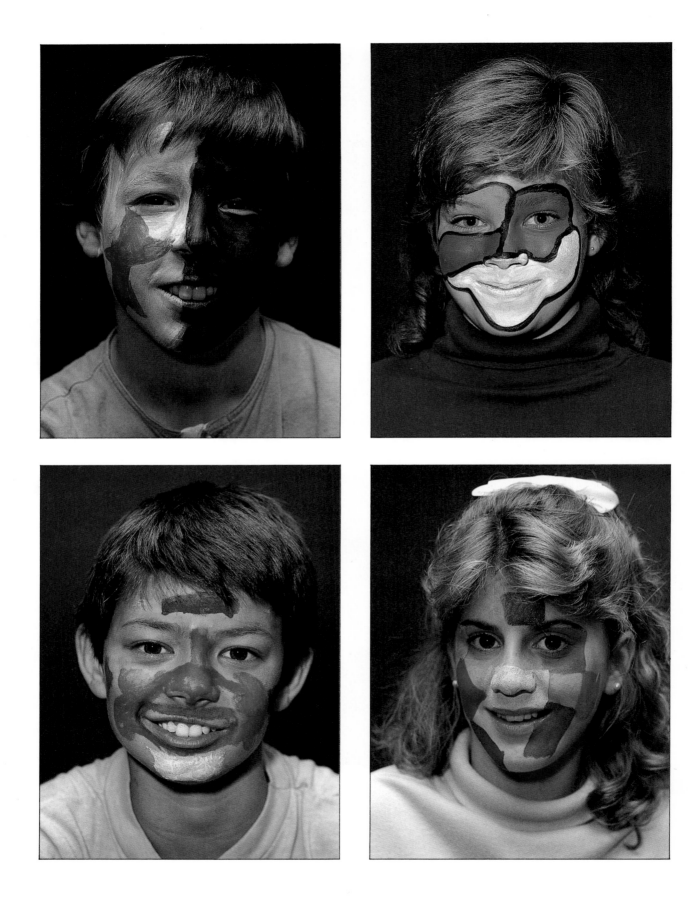

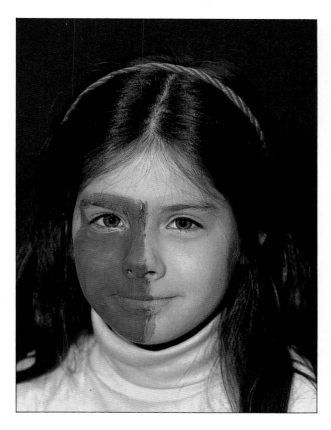

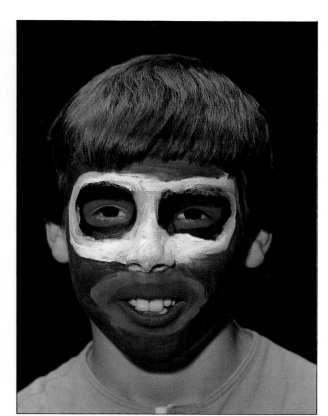

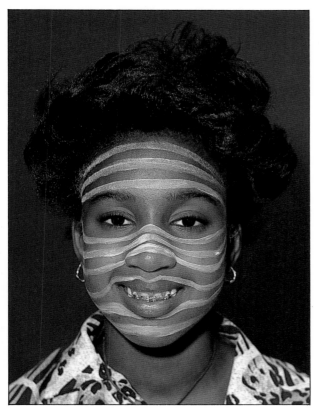

ANYTHING GOES

You can paint your face any way you like. You need only your imagination.

You can find inexpensive face-painting makeup in many kinds of places—toy stores, variety stores, or drugstores, for instance. Check at cosmetic counters; sometimes eye shadows are sold in a variety of colors and come in creams or sticks that are easy to apply.

Two suppliers from which you can order professional water-based makeup and greasepaint are listed below.

Columbia Stage and Screen Cosmetics
1440 North Gower Street
Hollywood, CA 90028
    (213) 464-7555

M.I.S. Retail Corporation
736 Seventh Avenue
New York, NY 10019
    (212) 765-8342